# READING BEAUTY

By Deborah Underwood

Illustrated by Meg Hunt

chronicle books · san francisco

Lex's bedroom brimmed with books;
she read them at top speed.
She even trained her puppy, Prince,
to fetch her things to read.

But on her fifteenth birthday,
Lex awoke—her books were gone!

She raced to find her parents.
"Make them stop! What's going on?"

They answered with a story:
"Long ago when you were small,
we held a celebration
and invited one and all."

"But while the guests were toasting you,
we heard a muffled shout.
A fairy burst in, furious
that she had been left out."

"How could you not invite me?
I must say, I'm rather miffed."
"But wait! We did—"
"Be quiet! Let me give your
Lex a gift."

"Like all you wretched readers,
Lex will live for reading—but!
When she's fifteen, she'll flip a page
and get a paper cut."

"The paper cut will bring a curse:
a death-like sleep will take her.
She'll stay that way forever—
only true love's kiss will wake her!"

"That's why we hid the books away,"
her mother said, dejected,
"for any book could cut you,
and you need to be protected."

Without its books, their world grew bleak,
consumed by dark and gloom.
Lex watched the shadows spreading
from the windows in her room.

"It's all my fault!" she said to Prince.
"I can't let things get worse!
I'll fly to find the fairy, then
I'll make her break the curse."

Prince's nose picked up a scent.
"Good dog! Those books—I need them!
We'll bring a bot to pack them up
and hold them while I read them."

Lex started off with *How to Fly*
then *How to Find a Fairy*,
and stories gave her courage when
the trip got rough and scary.

Meanwhile, in her fairy lair,
the fairy shrieked, "It's Lex!
She won't get me—I'll stop her with
the Thorny Hedges Hex."

"A wall of thorns around her home!
Nice try, but she can't hide."
A garden book helped Lex cook up
a homemade herbicide.

The hedge dissolved to shriveled
bits, so Lex and Prince could land.
The fairy said, "That girl is doomed.
I've something special planned!"

"I'll tempt her with the thing she loves:
a gorgeous, poisoned book
entitled *How to Lift a Curse*.
She'll have to take a look!"

## Zapzip!
A glowing book appeared.
Prince sniffed. "What's this?" Lex said.

HOW TO
Lift a
Curse

The fairy listened through the door.
"No sounds—she must be dead!"

The fairy inched near sleeping Lex,
to check her now-closed eyes,

But Lex sprang up and grabbed
her wand and said,
"Hello! Surprise!

I got quite good at faking sleep
when I was just a kid,
so I could read past bedtime.

"That curse will last forever!
You will never change my mind!"
Then Prince nudged Lex's leg and barked.
Lex looked. "What did you find?"

"You *were* invited to my ball!
We thought this didn't reach you!

Wait!
Can it be . . .
that you can't read?
Don't worry!

I will teach you!"

"Me? Read?"
In her excitement,
the poor fairy didn't think.
She touched the book, she turned
ghost-white,
and crumpled in a blink.

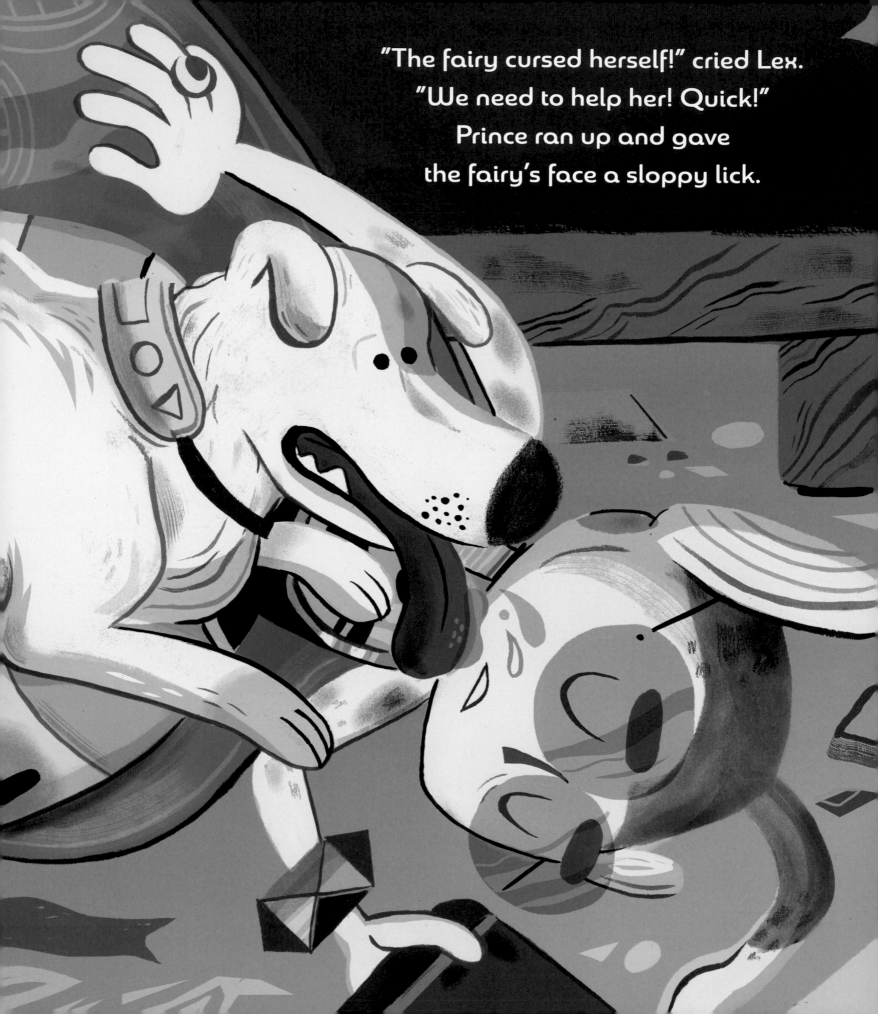

"The fairy cursed herself!" cried Lex.
"We need to help her! Quick!"
Prince ran up and gave
the fairy's face a sloppy lick.

The fairy slowly came to life.
"What happened? I'm not dead!"
"Oh, Prince loves everyone," Lex shrugged.
She smiled and scratched his head.

So Lex came home, the books came back,
the land was filled with laughter,

the fairy found a job,

and all read happily
ever after.

To Katherine —D. U.

For Mom, and in memory of Ann —M. H.

Library of Congress Cataloging-in-Publication Data available.

ISBN 978-1-4521-7129-6

Manufactured in China.

Design by Jennifer Tolo Pierce.

Typeset in Sangli.

The illustrations in this book were rendered in brush and ink, pastel,

marker, and graphite, and colored digitally.

10 9 8 7 6 5 4 3 2 1

Chronicle books and gifts are available at special quantity discounts

to corporations, professional associations, literacy programs, and

other organizations. For details and discount information, please contact

our premiums department at corporatesales@chroniclebooks.com

or at 1-800-759-0190.

Chronicle Books LLC

680 Second Street

San Francisco, California 94107

Chronicle Books—we see things differently. Become

part of our community at www.chroniclekids.com.